RIDGE, 1875

Twenty-One Elephants

by Phil Bildner

illustrated by LeUyen Pham

Simon & Schuster Books for Young Readers

NEW YORK   LONDON   TORONTO   SYDNEY

SIMON & SCHUSTER BOOKS FOR YOUNG READERS
An imprint of Simon & Schuster Children's Publishing Division
1230 Avenue of the Americas, New York, New York 10020
Text copyright © 2004 by Phil Bildner
Illustrations copyright © 2004 by LeUyen Pham

SIMON & SCHUSTER BOOKS FOR YOUNG READERS is a trademark of Simon & Schuster, Inc.
Book design by Dan Potash
The text for this book is set in Key.
The illustrations for this book are rendered in watercolor.
Manufactured in China
2 4 6 8 10 9 7 5 3 1
Library of Congress Cataloging-in-Publication Data • Twenty-one elephants / Phil Bildner ;
illustrated by LeUyen Pham.— 1st ed. p. cm. • Summary: Eight-year-old Hannah, upon completion
of the Brooklyn Bridge, enlists the help of P. T. Barnum and his twenty-one elephants to prove to
her father and all of Brooklyn that the bridge is safe. • ISBN 0-689-87011-6 (hardcover) •
1. Brooklyn Bridge (New York, N.Y.)—History—Juvenile fiction. 2. Barnum, P. T. (Phineas
Taylor), 1810–1891—Juvenile fiction. [1. Brooklyn Bridge (New York, N.Y.)—History—Fiction.
2. Barnum, P. T. (Phineas Taylor), 1810–1891—Fiction. 3. Jumbo (Elephant)—Fiction.
4. Elephants—Fiction.] I. Pham, LeUyen, ill. II. Title.
PZ7.B4923Twe 2004 • [E]—dc22 • 2004000349

Of course, this book is for a very special Hannah, Hannah Redmond Flannery.

This is also for Orlando Reece, who loved the story the moment it was born.

Big thanks and mad props to Eliza Kate Wicks-Arshack for her amazing research.

—P. B.

Many thanks go out to Melanie Cecka, my Brooklynite connection and sweet friend
who helped me cross the Brooklyn Bridge for the first time, and Dan Potash and
Emily Thomas, who took a chance and let me join their circus.

To my big brother, Dung Pham, the New Yorker, this book is humbly dedicated.

—L. P.

E ver since she was a little, little girl, Hannah watched the workers build the first steel suspension bridge in the whole world, the Brooklyn Bridge. She dreamed of the day when she would finally be able to walk across it and out into the big city.

When she was two, she waved to the enormous towers rising from the waters. When she was three, she pointed to the traveler rope as it first stretched across the river.

When she was five, she watched and wondered as the workers spun the four great cables. When she was eight, she gazed and gaped as they suspended the floor beams.

Hannah's father loved his little girl dearly, but he always clutched her hand a little tighter and drew in his breath a little deeper whenever she peered out at the modern marvel.

And when that day finally arrived and at long last the Brooklyn Bridge was complete . . .

"No little girl of mine will cross that metal monster!" her father declared as he waved and pointed to the nearly six-thousand-foot-long structure that now spanned the East River. Then he added: "Anything that stretches that long and rises that tall can't possibly be safe!"

When Chester A. Arthur, the twenty-first president of the United States, stood on the bridge alongside the governor of New York and the mayor of New York City, and pronounced it the Eighth Wonder of the World, Hannah thought for sure her father would finally come to his senses.

But he simply folded his arms, scratched his chin, and shook his head.

No, not even the commander in chief could change his mind.

When Mrs. Emily Roebling, the bridge's chief engineer, took the first ride across the bridge with a rooster—the symbol of victory—Hannah thought for sure her father would see the light.

But he simply folded his arms, scratched his chin, and shook his head.

No, not even the woman who had supervised the last years of the entire project could change his mind.

Yet Hannah refused to give up. There had to be a way to show her father all the marvels of the Brooklyn Bridge. There also had to be a way to convince him that it was strong and safe.

Hannah started with her family.

"It's too long!" cried her cousin.

"It's too tall!" said her grandma.

"If you ask me," added her aunt, "it's certain to collapse. That bridge looks like nothing more than a bunch of cardboard boxes tied together with string."

"With all due respect," Hannah said, because she couldn't be impolite, "the towers are made of granite, and there's over fourteen thousand miles of wire. Together it all weighs fourteen thousand six hundred eighty tons."

"Well, I'd first power the Fulton Street Ferry with my fists and feet before going over that bridge!" her uncle announced.

And everyone laughed.

Hannah tried school next.

"It's too long!" cried her teacher.

"It's too tall!" said her classmates.

"If you ask me," added the librarian, "it's certain to collapse. That bridge isn't strong enough for all that hustle and bustle, back and forth. A small town like Brooklyn has no business connecting itself to a big city like Manhattan."

"With all due respect," Hannah said, because she couldn't be impolite, "Brooklyn is hardly a small town. Over four hundred thousand people live here. Brooklyn is the third largest city in America. And with Brooklyn now connected to Manhattan, New York City could one day become the capital of the world."

"Well, I'd first swim across the river—and I float like a rock—before traversing that contraption!" her principal announced.

And everyone laughed.

Then Hannah went to the market by the church.

"It's too long!" cried the woman at the fruit stand.

"It's too tall!" said the policeman on patrol.

"If you ask me," added the man selling spices, "it's certain to collapse. It's too wide. One lane is all you need. Maybe two at the most."

"With all due respect," Hannah said, because she couldn't be impolite, "the Brooklyn Bridge needs all five lanes. The two outer lanes are for horse-drawn carriages, the two middle lanes are for the cable trains, and the fifth lane is for pedestrians like you and me."

"Well, I'd first walk on water before I'd walk on that bridge!" announced the minister.

And everyone laughed.

Now Hannah was sad.

Why did everyone agree with her father? Why was she the only one who wasn't afraid to walk across the Brooklyn Bridge? Why didn't anyone else share her dream?

Hannah's father couldn't stand to see his little girl so down. He knew the one thing that would cheer her up. . . .

The circus!

This year P. T. Barnum's Greatest Show on Earth had an added attraction—a herd of twenty-one elephants! And leading the herd of twenty-one elephants was Jumbo, the world's largest elephant.

Well, the moment Jumbo and his herd of elephants walked into the Big Top, *the* idea popped into Hannah's head.

Now, Hannah knew Mr. Barnum was a very busy man—probably much too busy to help out a little girl with a big problem—but Hannah also knew this was her *only* chance.

She waited until the last juggler stopped juggling and the last clown stopped clowning.

"Mr. Barnum!" she called. "Mr. Barnum!"

Mr. Barnum walked to the edge of the ring. "What can I do for you, little lady?"

"Pardon me, Mr. Barnum. Can I please borrow your twenty-one elephants?"

"Why ever would you want to borrow my twenty-one elephants, little lady?"

"Well, Mr. Barnum," Hannah replied, "if you must know, and I suppose you must since they are your elephants . . ." Hannah took a deep breath, clutched her father's hand as tight as she could, and explained her idea.

When she finished, Mr. Barnum folded his arms, scratched his chin, and *nodded* his head.

"Great minds think alike, little lady." Mr. Barnum reached into his pocket and handed her a flyer. "There's no need for you to borrow Jumbo or any of my twenty-one elephants. This is hot off the press. Start spreading the news!"

A few mornings later Hannah was up bright and early. She made sure everyone else was too.

"Come see! Come see!" She ran through her house.

"Come quick! Come quick!" She ran to the schoolhouse and the marketplace, too.

"Everyone, look!"

And there for all of Brooklyn to see was a sight almost too amazing to believe.

Yes, Hannah had finally found the way to prove to her father—and everyone in Brooklyn, for that matter—that the bridge was indeed safe and strong.

And from that day forth, Hannah and her father walked across the Brooklyn Bridge as often as they could.

Author's Note

Yes, P. T. Barnum did indeed march Jumbo and a parade of circus elephants across the Brooklyn Bridge on the spring evening of May 17, 1884.

By then the bridge had been open for almost a year, and many traveled across regularly. In fact, thousands of pedestrians and hundreds of vehicles crossed the bridge on the very first day, and within months of its opening, the first passenger train was already making scheduled trips.

However, an overwhelming number of Brooklynites still refused to traverse the bridge, and undoubtedly, the events of the previous Memorial Day had much to do with that.

Just days after the bridge officially opened, a woman tripped while climbing the steps onto the bridge. A nearby pedestrian screamed, and instantly, a rumor spread that the bridge was on the verge of collapse. A horrible stampede ensued, and in the resulting panic, a dozen people were killed and many more were seriously injured.

Politicians, engineers, and even Emily Roebling tried to reassure the uneasy citizenry, but more than ever, residents of Brooklyn feared the monolith which rose from the waters of the East River.

As the weeks and months passed, the skeptical public did begin to grow more accepting of the Brooklyn Bridge, but it was the greatest showman to ever walk the planet who finally laid to rest any and all lingering doubts and concerns.

As to what inspired P. T. Barnum to pull off, arguably, his greatest publicity stunt, who's to say? Surely, somewhere in Brooklyn, there must have been a little girl who saw the bridge as *her* opportunity. And who's to say that some little girl—some little Hannah—wasn't the source of his inspiration?

Did You Know?

Some people question whether Ms. Roebling was truly the bridge's chief engineer. John A. Roebling, the bridge's original chief engineer, died shortly after construction on the bridge had begun. His son, Washington Roebling, took over the project, but the younger Roebling was soon stricken by illness, which left him paralyzed and confined to his home. At that point his wife, Emily Roebling, assumed the leadership role, and there's little question she directed the project for the next decade.

If you'd like to see photographs and find out more factual information about the building of the Brooklyn Bridge, here are some sources that the author found very helpful:

Curlee, Lynn. *Brooklyn Bridge*, New York: Atheneum, 2001.

Mann, Elizabeth. *The Brooklyn Bridge: A Wonders of the World Book*, New York: Mikaya Press, 1996.

Shapiro, Mary, J. *A Picture History of the Brooklyn Bridge*, New York: Dover Publications Inc., 1983.

Snyder-Grenier, Ellen M. *Brooklyn!: An Illustrated History (Critical Perspectives on the Past)*, Philadelphia, PA.: Temple University Press, 1996.

Sutherland, Cora, A. *Bridges of New York City: The Museum of the City of New York*, New York: Barnes & Noble, 2003.